Printed in the USA

Running in Firefighter Boots

The Story of Duchenne Muscular Dystrophy

Written by Lipsy Patel
Illustrated by Eric M. Strong

To Mom, Dad, Sagar, Limca, Vikas, Shyla,
And to Jaylen and all the children who live with Duchenne muscular dystrophy

"Jaylen! Jaylen! Wake up, honey! Time for your first day of second grade."

"Ahhhhh, Mom! I don't want to go. Can I just stay home with you until next year?"

"Honey, we talked about this. This new school is going to be just like your old one, but with different kids. I'm sure you'll get along with them just fine."

As Mom was talking, Jaylen slowly got up from bed and took the Velcro off his moon boots, or foot orthotics, as the doctor called them. He didn't like wearing them, but he had no choice but to put them back on every night.

"I'm scared they're not going to like me. What if they ask me questions about why I can't do things like the other kids? Why did we have to move to a different school in the middle of the year?"

Jaylen's mom gave him a kiss on the forehead. "Jaylen, we've talked about this before. You're a strong boy, and I know the children in this new school will have questions about why you're different. If you tell them openly about why you can't do some things, I'm positive they'll understand."

There was no way out of it. Jaylen sighed loudly, walked slowly over to the bathroom, and got ready for the day.

Breakfast was quick, and then it was time for Jaylen's morning medicine. He once refused to take it, but now it was automatic. Nine pills every day, the faster the better. As he finished, his sister Shyla ran out of the door to get on the school bus.

"Mom, why does Shyla get to take the bus on her first day, and I don't?"

Mom stood quietly as her daughter ran off to the bus. She held Jaylen tight and gave him the biggest bear hug. "Because Mommy is going to drive you to school. Tell you what! We can play the US capital game as I drive you. How does that sound?"

Jaylen smiled his big smile and screamed, "Yes! Let's go!"

The drive to school was short. As they approached the front steps, Mom picked Jaylen up and carried him up the five steps to the front door. When she put him down, she glanced over to the right and noticed the ramp on the side. *Next time*, she thought, *I'll use that.*

Children were piling into the auditorium, waiting to be picked up by their classroom teachers. "Mom," Jaylen whispered, "do I have to go in there?"

"Yes, Jaylen, but today, we are going to visit the physical therapist and the principal first."

Principal Gibson and Jaylen's physical therapist, Ms. Booker, were in the office.
Both welcomed him with open arms.

After a few minutes of planning with the principal and therapist, all four walked down to Jaylen's new second grade classroom. From the outside, he could hear the sounds of children happily shouting to each other. "Why so loud?" asked Mom.

"Oh," Principal Gibson said, "that's probably because they're on a break before gym class."

At the sound of the word *gym*, Jaylen froze and looked directly at his mother.
"I hate gym class, Mom."

The classroom door was slightly ajar. As Jaylen walked in, no one stopped to see who was at the door—except for one student, who had been silently reading through the commotion.

The teacher, Mrs. Fisher, and Jaylen's one-on-one aide, Mrs. Deecan, were expecting him. Jaylen was taken to a seat in front of the room by his aide. As he was getting settled in, Mrs. Fisher spoke to the class. "Boys and girls, can I please have your attention? Before gym class, we are going to sit down at circle to meet our new student."

Again, Jaylen froze. Sitting down on the ground and getting up took extra work.

"Excuse me, Mrs. Fisher. Just a word."

Mrs. Fisher knew exactly what was worrying Jaylen's mom, Mrs. Jhaveri. Before Jaylen's mom could pull her aside, Mrs. Fisher smiled and said, "We have a chair set aside for him to sit at. Don't worry."

Mrs. Jhaveri was a bit surprised at the preparation done for her son, and very pleased. She left the classroom trusting that Jaylen was in good hands.

Mrs. Fisher didn't share why Jaylen was in the seat, but she spent a few minutes introducing him and encouraging other students to ask him questions.

Emma raised her hand and asked, "What's your favorite book?"

Brandon followed, asking, "What's your favorite TV show and video game?" Jaylen answered slowly, but with confidence.

The next question was from Matteo. "Hey, why are you sitting on a chair and not on the floor like the rest of us?"

Their teacher began to answer Matteo, but the bell rang; it was too late to continue. Mrs. Fisher told the class that they would continue with questions later. Jaylen walked nervously to the back of the already-forming line for gym class. It had been less than twenty minutes, and he already wanted to go home.

At gym class, the students were in the middle of a dodgeball tournament.

Balls, hitting! *Oh my*, Jaylen thought to himself. *This is the worst.*

Mr. McGregor, the gym teacher, didn't exactly know how to include Jaylen in the dodgeball tournament, so he let him stand along the sidelines with his aide and watch. During a break in the game, Manuel came up to him and asked curiously, "Hey, why are you just standing there?"

Once again, Jaylen was mute. He wanted to say something, but he didn't know how.

From the corner of Jaylen's eye, he could see the quiet child from earlier, Shane, watching him. Shane almost came up to him, which made Jaylen excited, but instead, Shane walked away.

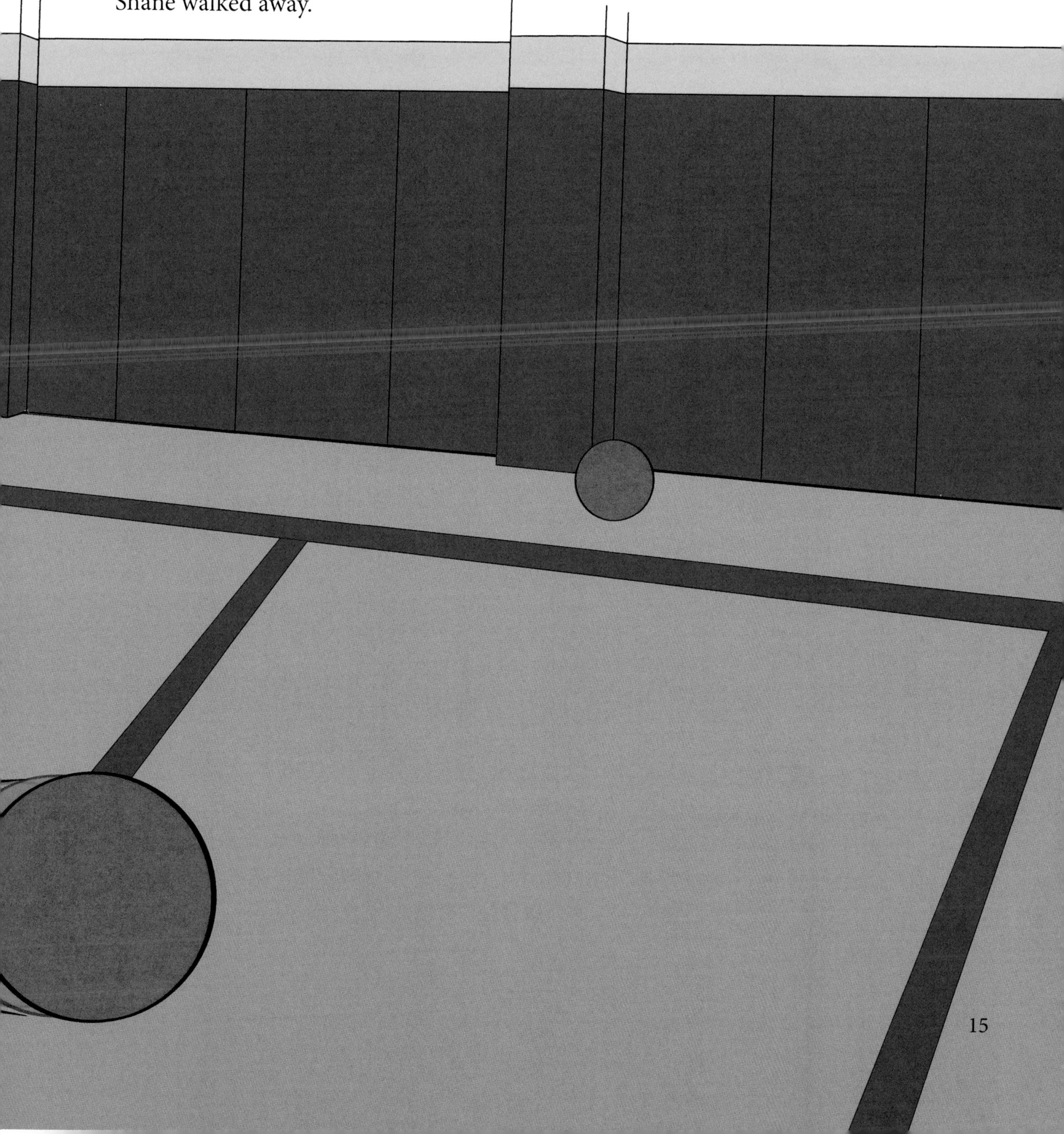

The rest of the day went by without any major hiccups. Jaylen was pleased. He just wanted to go home, play with his cars, and talk to Shyla. She never looked at him funny or asked him weird questions.

During dinner time, Mom and Dad asked Jaylen and Shyla about their days. Shyla couldn't stop talking about her new friend Jenna, but Jaylen was ignoring his parents.

"Jaylen, do you want to talk about your day?"

"No!"

"I'm sure there's one thing that went well today?" Dad said.

To that, Jaylen replied, "I feel like they think I'm weird. The kids keep asking me why I'm sitting on chairs and not playing dodgeball. It's embarrassing."

After finishing dinner, Mom and Dad spent some time discussing what to do. They knew that Jaylen's condition was not something to hide, and it made no sense for only the teachers to know. They agreed that the students needed to know as well.

Mom said, "Let me speak to Principal Gibson tomorrow and see if we can do something."

The next day at school, Mom met with Principal Gibson. She described their experience in Jaylen's previous school, and how they were able to share his condition with his classmates. It helped him feel included and prevented the same questions being asked over again by the students.

Principal Gibson listened and said, "I think that's a lovely idea. Being truthful and honest about what Jaylen is dealing with will allow the children to understand him better. I don't think the children are trying to be mean, but I do think they are curious." Mom agreed.

And so it was set. In the next week's gym class, Jaylen would be able to share his story in a unique way. That evening, when Mom told Jaylen the plan, there was a look of relief on his face. He walked over to his mom and gave her a hug.

The next week's gym class couldn't come fast enough. The adults stood on the sidelines while Jaylen walked nervously to the front of the class. Mom followed. She took out five sets of firefighter boots from a box she had borrowed from the local fire department. The children looked on with a little bit of confusion, but with wonder, too.

"Hello boys and girls! I am Mrs. Jhaveri, Jaylen's mom, and today Jaylen and I are going to show you how to play in an obstacle course. If you look around the gym, you'll see lots of courses for you and your classmates. Some areas have beanbags, and others have cones. Please raise your hand if you have done an obstacle course like this before."

Every hand in the room shot up. The kids loved obstacle courses. "Today, you are all going to do the same obstacle course that you do during Field Day, but with one exception," said Mrs. Jhaveri. "Once you are in five different teams, each person from each team will take a turn putting on the firefighter boots before taking on the course."

The children listened, but their faces were confused. They didn't understand why they had to wear the boots.

Jaylen didn't let their confusion upset him. He had already done this in his other school. Within minutes, the whistle blew and the race began. Children were attempting to run across the obstacle course with the boots, but it was much harder than it looked. Emma slipped. Matteo, the fastest child in the class, had a real hard time moving smoothly with the boots. One by one, students struggled through the course. Some children stopped and gave up, but the majority of the class did their best to finish.

After about twenty minutes of everyone getting a chance to try on the firefighter boots, the challenge was finally over. By this point, Jaylen and Mrs. Jhaveri were sitting on chairs. They asked the children to form a circle with them, and Mrs. Jhaveri asked the class questions. "Was that hard? How did you feel? Was anyone frustrated?"

The children participated, with all of them saying similar things. It was tiring, but they didn't want to give up. They had all tried their best.

Matteo burst out screaming, "That was the hardest thing ever!"

Jaylen listened to their answers. He was curious how they felt afterwards. That was his cue. Jaylen looked over to his classmates, all of them focused and quieting down. In a soft voice, he started. "My mom and I wanted to do this because we wanted to share something about me. When I started school, many of you asked me why I couldn't play dodgeball or sit on the floor during circle time."

"The reason I have to be careful with my body is because I have a disease called Duchenne muscular dystrophy. I know those are three very big words. They mean that I have trouble with my muscles, and I have a hard time moving as fast and quick as most children my age. You wore the boots so you can see how heavy my legs feel and how it's harder for me to move. I try my best, but sometimes, I have to slow down so I don't hurt myself. Duchenne muscular dystrophy stops me from being very active. I have to take medicine to keep me strong for now. One day, my muscles will not work and I will use a wheelchair." Jaylen paused slightly. "But I am still a normal kid and want to be included in things."

Jaylen stopped talking and waited. Several seconds went by until the quietest student in Jaylen's class, Shane, whispered, "I don't have weak muscles, but I am also different. I am much shier than everyone else, and it is hard for me to make friends. I can be your friend if you want."

One by one, every student in the class started talking about things they struggled with. Emma volunteered that she couldn't read and comprehend books well. Brandon shared that he didn't understand multiplication. Manuel said that he had a really hard time hearing, so his mom and dad were thinking of taking him to the doctor. In a matter of minutes, everyone was adding to the conversation.

33

Jaylen smiled at his class. His body relaxed and he felt at ease for the first time since he started second grade. He thought to himself, *maybe these kids can be my friends after all.*

There were a few minutes left until gym class was over. The conversation continued, but students started getting out of the circle and huddling around each another. Suddenly, Brandon jumped up and jogged over to Jaylen. He gave Jaylen a high five. One by one, every child did. Some students helped put the firefighter boots back in the box.

When the teacher asked that everyone line up, the students walked over to the line, playfully trying to cut one another to be first. Jaylen stood last in line out of habit with his aide—or so he thought.

When he turned around, his new friend Shane whispered, "I was waiting for you. You can go ahead of me."

About the Author

Lipsy dedicates this book to Jaylen and all children living with Duchenne muscular dystrophy. Her goal in writing this book is simple. Children's books can tell stories that help children (and adults) empathize and show compassion towards others with differences to them. She wants people to know Jaylen's story—and the stories of other children facing everyday challenges in a manner that enables families, teachers, and children to have honest and safe conversations together. Her goal is to write more books raising awareness about the many challenges different children face. This is her first book.

Lipsy received her degree in Elementary Education from Rutgers Graduate School of Education and went on to teach at both private Montessori and public elementary schools in New Jersey. Although she no longer teaches, she works regularly with schools and children for a learning company. She believes the number one priority in education should be to raise emotionally intelligent children who care about others.

Jaylen is her nephew, and they have a lot in common. Their favorite thing to do is stare at the world map and talk about different countries and where their next vacations will be. She refers to him as her Gremlin, and he likes to call her "Masy."

Made in the USA
Middletown, DE
22 November 2019